If you're a fan of paranormal romance/erotica, this novella is right up your alley! Just make sure you're never stuck in one with Masterson. He bites.

WE SO NERDY

Masterson is a deliciously dark but irresistibly romantic antihero and he completely captured my heart!

JUDY LEWIS

To Susan –

MASTERSON

A VAMPIRE SONS STORY

ELLIS LEIGH

Stay naughty

Ellis Leigh –

Kinship Press

Masterson: A Vampire Sons Story

Copyright © 2015 by Ellis Leigh

Kinship Press
PO Box 221
Prospect Heights, IL 60070

ISBN: 978-1-944336-22-6

INTRODUCTION

Masterson holds himself to the highest of standards, but a chance encounter with a human woman in the most mundane of places turns his world on end. What's a vampire to do when temptation for more than blood consumes him?

CHAPTER ONE

Saturday

"MASTERSON! SO GOOD TO SEE YOU, MY FRIEND."

Sliding my eyes in the direction of the fool yelling across the crowded room, I fought back the urge to scowl. He grinned in that way blusterous men do when they know they're outmatched, wrapped his arm around a dark-haired human who looked much like a plastic doll, and strode my way. Bold...ignorant and dangerous, but bold.

I nodded my head at the man in question, my only attempt at civility. A century ago, I would have knocked his ass through the wall for daring to invade my space. I thought about challenging him—teaching him a lesson in how our kind should behave around ones of a higher status—but his stupidity wasn't worth the time.

He stopped directly in front of me, watching. Waiting. Almost vibrating in excitement. I probably would have spoken to him, but I couldn't find it in me to worry about his name, or words, or giving a fuck. He was just one more low-level vamp in a room full of even lower level ones. A big fish in a little pond...but I was a fucking shark and had been for enough years to have grown exhausted with the necessity of interacting with others. Let them have their petty infighting and their battles for territory, for they had no idea how little it would all matter eventually. How little anything would truly matter.

Instead of dealing with no-name, I eyed the human on his arm. Letting enough of my inner vampire show to give her goose bumps, licking my lips as the hairs on her arm stood on end. Making sure I was sufficiently scary to warrant a reaction from her. Wishing she were able to entice a reaction from me. Idly wondering how long it would take for me to drain her blood simply to rid the world of her chemically altered, overprocessed scent.

Eyes locked with the human—wondering about but ignoring the small black ears perched atop her head— I'd almost forgotten about the intruding vamp until he inched closer, completely invading my space. His attention seemed too intense, too aggressive. He wanted something.

The no-name vamp shoved the human forward, his eyes alight. "I don't think you've met Ginger yet."

I didn't respond, having no fucking clue who Ginger was. When I continued to stare at him silently, he faltered and gestured to the woman with the cat ears.

"My human. The one—" He waved his hand, for some reason at odds with saying the words.

"The one you're pushing at me to what? Fuck right here on this couch?" I raised an eyebrow, the predator in me waking up as his face blanched and he nodded. "Also, I hadn't realized our pets needed names."

"Oh, well…" He shifted his weight, eyes bouncing from mine to the woman at his side. Completely transparent in his want to provide me with her services. What by all rights was mine as the highest-ranking vampire in the nest, though I had no interest in his little concubine.

"Sir, I wish to offer you Ginger as a sexual partner and blood host for the evening. She's been well-trained and would happily take care of you in any way you so desired." No-name's eye twitched, his face showing his every weakness. He cared for the girl but was following the doctrines of our kind. Interesting. His pet was definitely not the prey at this party, not with him so obvious in his desires. The bastard had become the toy to be batted, far more interesting than a human woman had ever been.

Finally, something to hold my attention.

I threw one arm over the back of the chair, casual, and waggled a finger at his pet. "Sit on my lap. Now."

The woman complied immediately, turning back to me and sitting with her legs spread across my thighs. She leaned back, pressing her ass against my cock. And then she began to swivel her hips. Once, twice, her hand running along her breast, the visual quite engaging, the rocking motion solid and sure.

Well-trained, indeed.

As my cock hardened beneath her, I pushed her hair over to one shoulder and leaned in. Perhaps a taste. It was my right after all. I let my vampire side shine through my eyes, felt the tingle as the whites went dark. Knowing they'd be fully black in seconds. Calling forth the beast within me.

"That's it, pet." I kissed her neck, ran my fangs up the side of her. Scenting her. But then I froze.

She smelled…drugged. Scared. Half-dead already.

"You dare to bring me an unwilling human?" I asked in a low voice, glaring at no-name, making sure he knew exactly how dangerous of a situation he was in. No-name startled, his own eyes wide but remaining light. Still passing for human instead of calling forth his vamp side. Idiot.

"No, no. Ginger is willing. Always. Let her show you."

I fisted my hand in the pet's hair and bent her head back, inhaling her scent, keeping my eyes locked on his. Using the power of my thrall, the ability to make creatures of any sort do exactly what I wanted them to, I stole his ability to move, leaving him helpless and weak as he watched me discover his lies.

His hands clasped and unclasped as he edged closer to me—to his pet. His intentions were clear, his need to protect his pet obvious. Fucking idiot. Every vamp in this place would be on her in a heartbeat if they knew she mattered to him. It was part of our nature, the urge to torment the weaker ones around us. No-name should have claimed his precious human with his bite, with his vampire essence, if he actually cared about the thing. Showing so much interest in an unclaimed human was the vampire equivalent of pouring chum into a sea of sharks. Irresistible. Especially to someone as old as I.

"Let her show me? I wasn't aware you'd earned a higher status than I, that you had the clout to make demands of me. Or did you forget what my name means? Did you forget who my sire is or how fucking long I've been doing as I pleased, while vampires like you crawled at my feet in the hopes of being gifted with the chance to do my bidding?"

My growl and raised eyebrow had him backpedaling, stumbling over his words, trying hard not to upset one of the Master's own.

"I meant no disrespect. I simply wanted to offer you something you might find enjoyable…sir."

Growling, I sat back and let the pet he called Ginger do her thing, her ass pressing hard on my deflated cock. But that fun only lasted a handful of seconds before I was bored again. I was too old to give a fuck about the newly changed vampires surrounding me, too experienced to take pleasure in some half-assed lap dance from a human without the skills to make it worthwhile and with too many drugs in her system to have any real sense of what she was doing.

I considered the pet, turning her head to truly see her for the first time all evening. Her eyes were glazed, empty of any emotion. Dark lips and eye makeup accentuated the paleness of her skin, distracting those who saw her from the truth. She was sickly, overused, and near the end of her life without even realizing it. I ran a finger down her cheek, over the odd black lines fanning out from her nose...lines she'd painted on for some reason. She continued her lap dance, still working my cock, refusing to stop even though I could sense she wanted to. Could feel her resistance.

"You know," I said, returning my attention to no-name, "she's not what I want."

I pushed her toward her keeper and rose to my feet, standing head and shoulders above the other vamp. Releasing my thrall, I allowed him to grab his little pet, a twinge in my gut telling me it was time to get the hell away from them. "If you're going to offer a concubine to those of us above your station, I would suggest you find one with better training. An unwilling woman is not what we desire, blood fouled by chemicals not what we need. And what is with that ridiculous headpiece and face paint it's wearing?"

No-name wrapped an arm around his pet, protective and obviously offended. "She happens to be the best concubine I've ever experienced. She takes the drugs to relax around our kind, as most humans do. And it's almost Halloween, sir. She's dressed as a kitty cat."

I hissed, rage boiling within me at his daring to argue. "Perhaps you and your pet should spend some time at the Master's nest in Paris. I'm sure he could teach you how to treat a proper concubine, as well as how not to speak to one of his sired sons."

No-name's jaw clenched, his eyes growing dark as he tightened his hold on his pet. Understanding my threat. My sire was a violent, demanding vampire, ancient even by our standards. He would sooner kill the vamp and his pet as a warning to the rest of the young ones than train them, and no-name knew it.

"I apologize," No-name said, biting out his words, his submission to me obviously a little bitter. "I don't believe a visit to your sire is required, sir. I will work on Ginger's training and make sure she's appropriately prepared for your next visit."

"No."

"No?"

I shook my head, eyeing the pet one last time. She could never be released, never allowed to return to her human life. No-name had gotten his taste of her blood and liked it. He'd follow her forever.

"Destroy her," I demanded, knowing a quick death was the best possible end for his little pet considering the situation. "I'll be expecting better if I dare to honor you with my presence again."

Ginger whined, but to no-name's credit, he didn't pull her closer or calm her. Instead, he held my gaze, firm in his stance. Learning, perhaps, though I doubted it. I'd have to remember to send out the Master's guards to ensure no-name complied with my order. To make sure his Ginger had been released from the hell she was currently enduring. I had no interest in coming back to this nest.

I walked away without saying another word, the entire incident nearly forgotten with my first step. I didn't weave through the crowd of humans and vampires. Instead, I used my thrall to move them out of my way, earning a number of hisses and growls from the ones not used to being pushed aside by a stronger vamp.

I was almost to the back door when another vamp approached, the name of this one quick to my tongue.

"Samuelson," I said, nodding once. Vampire Samuel was the Master's sired brother. He was also the only vampire allowed within my sire's private residence, aside from those of us with the Master's own bite mark on our throats. Vampire Samuel was a man to be respected. His name offered the vampires he created a modicum of that same respect. As my name afforded me the respect due the Master.

"Masterson. Where have you been? I haven't seen you in weeks."

"Weeks? Surely not." I tried to pinpoint the last time I'd run into the hulking vamp but couldn't. Every day blended together in my mind, leaving them all fuzzy and . A by-product of doing the exact same thing each day without interruption. Of a life of boredom.

"Getting a little feebleminded in your old age, man?" Samuelson asked, grinning. "Perhaps you need to partake of one of the concubines as a donor."

I scoffed. "The blood here is foul. Too many drugs being taken by the pets. I prefer my host blood to be clean."

"Well, good luck with that. Humans kept as concubines these days seem to require the drugs to allow our kind to feed. The two seem to go hand in hand." He scowled, his gaze dancing over the younger vamps in the room. "These bastards have no fucking clue. They think adrenaline and fear in the blood make it somehow better, but I disagree. The sweetness that comes from an aroused woman releasing her control to my touch, my teeth—" he closed his eyes and breathed deeply, practically moaning "—that's the true nectar of our kind. It's why I love Halloween so much… The women seem more willing to accept our oddities as an act for the season. Makes for good hunting of any kind."

His words made my empty stomach ache all the more, made my hands clench into fists as my cock twitched. Fuck, what I wouldn't give for the perfect host. Clean blood, a willing attitude, and a daringness that allowed my sexual appetite to be fulfilled. The ultimate partner.

"Too true, my friend." Anxious to leave, to hunt, to search out the impossible, I glanced at the door. "If you'll excuse me, I believe I'll be heading back to the city."

"Hunting tonight? I've heard the Carnival has been quite busy lately with the holiday crowds."

"Perhaps." I shrugged, playing off my need. Not willing to give him an ounce of anything to use against me or where I chose to hunt my prey. I could respect him as Samuel's sired son, someone almost my equal in the eyes of the Master, but that didn't mean I trusted him. As I knew he didn't actually trust me.

"Good luck to you, Masterson." He took a step back, his eyes darkening as they sought a pet to slake his thirst for the evening. "I hope you find whatever it is you're hunting for. We only have a week before

Halloween, and then we're back to hiding ourselves in the shadows."

"Good luck to you as well, Samuelson." Without a second thought, I hurried outside, dissolving into shadow the moment I walked through the door. I needed to get away. Between my lack of a meal and that half-assed lap dance no-name's pet had given me, I was completely on edge. Too hungry to do anything but think about finding a meal. Too horny to want to hunt. What I wouldn't give to find a donor human to claim and make mine. One to fuck and feed from at the same time. Someone a little daring, with soft curves and a willing mouth, clean blood, and a pussy to lose myself inside of. But that creature, that once plentiful pet, seemed to have become the Holy Grail of the vampire world. I'd been looking for close to six hundred years, across every continent where humans resided, for someone to be my donor and replace the one I'd lost. I'd been searching tirelessly for the one thing I might actually come alive for. The one thing that could possibly wake me up. And I had failed, miserably and repeatedly.

As I took flight, nothing more than a deeper shade of darkness soaring across the sky, I wondered if I would ever succeed.

CHAPTER TWO

Sunday

THE WOMAN WALKED WITH PURPOSE, HER STRIDE long and her steps sharp. The scent of her excitement trailed delicately along the breeze, enticing me to follow as she led the way to her apartment building. Her scuffed high heels clacked against the concrete, the noise loud against an otherwise quiet city street. The rhythm of her impending death.

I moved to walk beside her, grabbing her hand, a human act of possession I'd become somewhat fond of over the years. She looked up through her multicolored, fake lashes, trying to appear seductive, I assumed. Perhaps that expression worked with human men who seemed to be led by their dicks instead of their brains. Not me, though. I saw through her and the silly costume she wore.

Still, I pasted a smile on my lips, too hungry for

more than a half-assed effort, more than ready to end this charade. I'd had enough of her banal conversation and mediocre attempts at flirting. But I played my part, pretending to be solely focused on bedding her. Allowing her to dictate the hows and the wheres. She thought she was running this game; that the power play between us would lead to a night of sex with a stranger on her terms. She thought she was in control. I almost couldn't wait to prove her wrong.

When we reached her building, I thralled her enough to urge her to turn into the unlit gangway between buildings. She obeyed the mental nudge as I expected, heading for the dark back door instead of the safer, better-lit front entrance. Her striped tights nearly glowed, her short white dress cut just high enough to showcase a pair of frilly panties. I had no idea what sort of pop-culture persona she was impersonating, but it didn't work for me. Too childish, too ridiculous. But she was warm and drug-free from what I could tell, so I would make some use of her.

She giggled, mumbling about never using her rear entrance, trying to be funny with some kind of anal sex innuendo. I didn't pay attention, though. Too obsessed with the darkness and the privacy the location afforded me while still being exposed to the possibility of being seen or heard. Ready to take what I'd been working for all evening, knowing this was the place to close this deal.

My time had come.

As she stumbled over the uneven walkway, I jumped, grabbing her with one arm and yanking her off her feet. She didn't struggle, didn't realize my intentions…and she never would. I struck before she could give in to her fear, biting hard and fast. Plunging deep into her warm, soft flesh. Finding her wet and ready for me, I bit down harder. Taking more. With my teeth completely buried in her neck, her skin and muscles tore at my eagerness. And still she didn't struggle, didn't resist. I moved too fast, ready to thrall her if need be, hoping I wouldn't have to.

Pulling her body against mine, I groaned and filled my mouth with her blood. Every drop a gift, every ounce gulped down my throat something precious. Fuck, she tasted divine. Sweet and slightly tart, like early-season cherries. No drugs to make her blood bitter, no fear to bite back at me with its acid-like aftertaste. Simple and pure, only slightly dulled by the effects of the earlier thrall. So close to being exactly the taste I'd been searching for. So close…but yet not.

Arm around her shoulder, I pinned her to me as I continued feeding from her neck. One long pull, two, blood rushing over my tongue and down. Filling me, warming me from the inside. My cock hardened and my vision cleared as my eyes went black, every inch of my body feeling the power her blood infused me with. She shivered, trembled as I held her. Began to quake as I took more, took too much, took it all. Close, so close, almost what I wanted, definitely part of what I needed.

I clung tighter, letting my teeth lengthen that final bit, moving my tongue over her flesh slowly as the blood became harder to pull. As I drained her.

Fangs deep in her neck, my body practically

wrapped around hers, I sucked out every bit. Taking the blood from her, but only the blood. I fought back the urge to grind my hard cock against her ass as I fed, knowing it would break the calm I'd surrounded her in. That it would taint the last of her blood with the acidic flavor of her fear. She was my meal, nothing more.

But I wanted to fuck, to find release. As the blood warmed my belly, I yearned for that extra satiation. Sadly, my little Cherry was not the one to balance both sides of my needs. She was far too reserved for a man with my particular tastes. Too nervous to let my hands wander in the restaurant where I'd charmed and seduced her. Too shy to entertain the notion of flipping up her skirt for me in the bathroom because of the possibility that others might hear us. She'd wanted safe and private, and that need had led us to her apartment building alone. Silly woman. The prudish desire to keep her sex life under wraps had led to her death. I preferred my women more daring, more willing. And I was much more likely to leave a sexual partner alive than to drink from her.

So I'd allowed her to lead me to her home, knowing I'd only take her blood. The fear she'd experience if I pushed for what I really wanted, if I coerced myself into her pussy even as I thralled her to stay relaxed, would taint the sweetness. Some vampires liked that sort of thing, liked taking what wasn't offered and the burn that fear brought to the blood. I was not one of those men. I liked my women compliant, aroused, and completely consenting. It made the blood that much sweeter. Made them ripe and juicy to my tongue, like fruit right off the tree. I wanted my women fighting to pull me in deeper, to truly want my cock buried inside of them, not to push me off them.

With a final sigh, she stilled in my arms, her quaking over, her life as well. I didn't stop drinking her down, though. Needing more, making sure to take every single drop. Finally pressing my cock against her ass to relieve a little of the pressure building inside me.

When I'd completely drained her, I dropped the body to the stone path. She looked like a doll, a broken, dirtied doll left behind on the side of the road. An intriguing image for sure. I pulled out my cock with a groan. I couldn't leave her to be found, not in this day and age. Too many humans believed in vampires, too many records existed to track oddities such as dead bodies appearing without blood within them. Cherry would need to be disposed of properly.

But first, I needed to find release.

Growling, wishing for much more than my own hand, I worked my cock in the shadows of the gangway. Pulling, tugging, and twisting the hardened flesh until my balls pulled up tight to my body, until my knees shook with the need to get to that final edge. Until I roared and came in spurts along the brick wall, slowing my strokes, drawing it out.

Leaning against the opposite building, I took a few deep breaths as my hand lazily rubbed the length of my cock. Still hard…still wanting. Never truly satisfied. Giving up on the idea of another self-induced orgasm, I cracked my neck and stood to my full height once more. I'd gotten my fill of blood, but that had only made me want something more. Want to find another woman, a willing one to fuck. To bury my cock in her instead of my teeth, preferably someplace a little naughty, a little exposed. Cherry had made me desire a different kind of meal. I'd be hunting again…and soon.

When I'd made myself presentable once more, I picked up Cherry's body. It was a long way to where I needed to go, and I didn't want to end up relegated to human modes of transportation once the sun came up. Dissolving into the deepest shadows, taking Cherry's body with me into the nothing, I hopped from dark spot to dark spot, making my way out into the desert where a clan of vampires kept a small incinerator-like hole for burning the bodies we drained. Where I could dispose of Cherry before searching for the next woman, hunt for the possibility of a quick fuck to take the edge off.

Before I set about looking for that elusive donor.

CHAPTER THREE

Monday

THE FILTH OF THE CITY DISGUSTED ME, ESPECIALLY in the golden light of a dawning day, but I stayed because it offered me the perfect place to hide. The higher the population in one metropolitan area, the more crime the region experienced. Humans could be violent with each other, and sometimes they disappeared without a trace. These facts were good for me because I killed enough of them to attract serious attention in smaller towns. Not that I had to kill any of them, really. I could only take what I needed, leave them wobbly and unsure of what happened, unable to remember me. But then they'd be in my head for the rest of their lives. Their blood would call to me, force me to seek them out for another taste, keep my emotions tied to theirs until the day they finally died and set me free.

I hadn't left a human alive in over six hundred years, not since the first woman I used for both sex and blood, the closest thing to a donor I'd ever encountered. She'd been special, not my ideal but as close to perfection as I could find. Like a dark-colored peach sitting high in the treetops, juicy and ripe, waiting for my bite to pierce its delicate skin and suckle its sweetness. Peaches may not have been my favorite—I much preferred plums or figs —but they were good enough for the moment. Just as she had been.

Peaches had stayed with me for only four months, her body willingly given, her blood what fed me. She'd been mine, claimed, completely safe from the vampires who sat lower than I on the social standing at the Master's court unless I chose to share her. And I did share her—both her blood and her sex. Too much, apparently.

My maker had murdered her in front of me to teach me a lesson, tainting that sweet blood with her terror, spilling it all over the floor for a transgression I could no longer remember. Something about place and standing, about allowing what should have been mine to be made common. Something about protecting the Master's name. A lesson cemented into my consciousness.

And so I'd left, found new lands, and searched for another to replace my Peaches. Centuries later, I was still searching.

Lost in my memories, I missed my block, ending up on a section of the street I normally avoided due to its traffic. Orange pumpkins and black bats decorated store windows, purple witch shoes near the doors. Halloween was coming, and these humans seemed to welcome it in an almost childlike way. Disgusting.

I was about to turn around to head back to my nest when a scent on the wind made me stop. My body locked down, frozen in want and anticipation at the aroma. Subtle and delicious, carrying with it hints of things that made me hard and hungry at the same time. Dark things…deliciously sinful things. The scent of things long dead lingered underneath the sweetness, something I found intriguing. Shaking off my surprise, I sniffed, tracking the scent. Wanting it. Craving a taste of it.

The scent culminated at a local coffee shop, one of those overpriced places humans patronized for the ambiance instead of the actual coffee. Not that I cared where I was, so long as I found what I was searching for. I yanked open the door, barely noticing the fake spider web-covered windows and paper bats hanging from the ceiling. Nearly crazed with my need to locate the source of that scent.

Then I did…and my long-dead heart nearly came back to life.

Tall and tan, with round hips that drew my eyes like a magnet, she stood in line, waiting her turn to order her stimulant of choice. Skintight, stretchy black fabric molded to her legs, accentuating every curve, turning her ass from something I simply wanted to stare at to something I desperately wanted to bite. But that couldn't distract me from her scent. Warm and syrupy, honeyed almost, with a slightly rancid undertone that called to the basest parts of me. A scent made to entice a vampire like me.

I stepped behind her, too close for social norms, unable to resist my draw to her. Either unaware of my proximity or ignoring my rudeness, she sighed and yanked on her messy bun. I nearly closed my eyes in bliss as her scent intensified, my cock growing rock hard in my trousers. Death teased me, tickled my nose, caused my fangs to descend and my mouth to water. But with the dark came the light, soft and sugary melding with the harsh and putrid. She smelled fruitlike and sweet. Almost too sweet, the rot tempering the cloying. Fuck, what I wouldn't give to touch, to taste, to devour. To have that scent on my tongue, to swallow it down. To bury my cock inside her as I drank every drop of whatever caused that natural perfume.

She glanced over her shoulder, peering into my eyes for a brief moment, hers going wide as she took me in. That was all I needed. Dark and deep, soulful eyes met mine, and I practically purred. She was as beautiful as she smelled, as intriguing as that mixed aroma seeping from her pores. Sexy in her casualness, natural and pure instead of processed. I wanted to grab her, kiss her, slide inside her. But instead, I smiled, keeping it small, hiding my teeth and attempting to temper my normal predator aura. Refusing to scare the first human I'd actually taken notice of in decades.

"Busy today," I murmured, keeping my voice low and relaxed. Very human.

She glanced behind me to where three more people

stood waiting. Accepting my position and opinion with a shrug. "It's Monday."

"Yes." I scanned the strategically lit shop, wondering why its being a Monday mattered in the number of customers. Too far removed from human interaction to pick up those subtle social cues. "I guess it is."

"What are you drinking, hun?" the barista asked, watching the two of us with one eye, her other covered in a patch. A pirate costume, I assumed. I didn't respond to her, waiting for the lovely human now standing beside me to place her order.

Smiling, giving me a sexy look that made me want to fuck her right there on the counter beside the cash register, my little obsession turned toward the costumed woman behind the counter, ordering something warm and milky. Probably something sweet. She bent forward just so, her ass in the air and her hips tilted in a way that pulled a low growl from my throat. With her at that height and angle, I knew I could slide inside her without even bending my knees. Perfect.

But then she straightened, stepping away, stealing that particular fantasy. When it was my turn at the counter, I ordered an espresso before edging over to the pickup area. Never taking my eyes off that messy bun as it bobbed above most of the other heads. Thankful for the crowd, I again moved too close to my target, enticed by the scent rolling off her still. Intrigued. Thoroughly obsessed.

She smelled like plums, my favorite fruit from my human days, something that had stuck with me through all my years.

"Sorry," I said quietly as I inched closer, her arm brushing my chest. "It's quite crowded."

"No problem." She shrugged and fingered the bottom hem of her gray jacket, adjusted the backpack tossed casually over her shoulder. An act that made me want to look inside the hideous bag, see what she was hiding, what she was doing in her life. No colleges were located within walking distance, so she probably wasn't a student. Her wardrobe choice didn't seem professional like so many of the others in this infernal place. She was dressed casually, with sneakers on her feet and no makeup on her face, standing out in a sea of unflattering skirts and shapeless suit coats. And I'd never seen anything more beautiful.

"Do you come here often?" I asked, nearly groaning as she turned those sinful eyes my way.

Her eyebrow went up, a mocking smile twisting one side of her mouth. "Did you really just use that line?"

I huffed a small laugh and shook my head, playing off her response, unsure what was wrong with my question. "Yes, I suppose I did. My apologies. I'm new to the area and was simply trying to be polite."

She watched me, almost wary in her observation, but still smiling. "I come here quite often, then. It's the best coffee shop on my way to work."

"Ah, well, perhaps—"

Sadly, a man behind the counter interrupted me, his voice booming through the buzz of the crowd around us. "Large latte, extra shot, three sugars."

"That's me." She grabbed her cup before turning my way once more, her eyes sliding over my body in a seductive inspection before she headed for the door. "See you around, new guy."

She left in a rush, escaping before I could react, leaving me hard and wanting. And completely confused over what had just happened.

"Espresso."

I spun toward the exit, desperate to track her but not wanting to scare her. Forcing myself to settle down before I made a mistake or came off looking like a fool. Knowing where I could find her again.

"Espresso? Sir…your drink."

Pushing through the door and out into the cool morning air, I strode down the street in the opposite direction of my quarry. Patience…I needed to exercise patience. But for the first time that I could remember, I found myself excited about what would happen the next day. There was possibility on the air, potential to finally acquire what I'd been looking for. The scent, the eyes, the sensuality that screamed through her every movement…I had to get a taste of her, a feel for her body. I needed to know everything about her.

I needed to bite into that delectable plum.

But not yet. I'd find her again, and soon, but I would wait until tomorrow. After all, it was only Monday.

CHAPTER FOUR

Tuesday

On Tuesday, I swept into the coffee shop shortly after they opened. I didn't want to miss the opportunity to observe my Plum once more. For hours, I sat and waited, a cooling espresso sitting untouched on the table in front of me. Watching as the humans came and went, as the bats overhead fluttered each time the door opened. As the customers laughed and pointed at the garish decorations. I hadn't paid so much attention to the population around me in years, hadn't bothered to try to understand their subculture and social cues. But I studied them now, attempting to learn how to behave around Plum. What might make her willing to interact with me, to attract her to me.

Before her, I'd thrall a woman just enough to make her compliant to my advances, a power that diluted the sweetness of her blood and left me disappointed. I didn't want that for Plum. Didn't want to negate that inherent sweetness I'd scented yesterday. But it was more than her blood I was after. More than the idea of burying myself inside her, too. Something about her intrigued me too much for my usual disregard. I wanted to determine what drew me to her before I took what I needed. What I craved.

And then she was there, walking through the door, smiling as she took in the bats fluttering overhead. As she turned toward the counter, she caught my eye. I smiled, fighting the urge to run to her, sweep her into my arms and bite that long neck of hers. Humans were not so forward, I'd learned, so I waited, keeping my eyes on her. Tracking my prey. My Plum caught me watching as she ordered her coffee, giving me a sassy little smirk over her shoulder. A sensuous look that had me shifting in my chair as I grew hard and uncomfortable. As my cock swelled and my thoughts turned from biting her to fucking her against the counter. Or possibly across one of the tables. Perhaps she'd be more reserved, requiring a modicum of privacy. I could fuck her in the public restroom at the back of the establishment. That was an intriguing thought. I would bend her over the sink, spread her legs with my feet, and watch her face in the mirror as she came around my cock. I'd make her cry out my name as the other patrons pretended not to hear our coupling. But they would, they'd hear it, and they'd be turned on by the sounds we'd make together.

Intriguing indeed.

Distracted, I barely caught Plum's eye as she headed

toward the door. I sat up straight, peering at her, giving her my full attention. She slowed, watching me as I watched her, her sweet, warm beverage clutched in her hands.

"Good morning," I said, allowing one side of my mouth to turn up.

She smiled, a seductive glimmer in her eye. "Good morning, new guy. Happy Tuesday."

"It is indeed."

She licked her bottom lip and tugged it between her teeth, ducking her head just a bit. Shy young girl and experienced seductress all at once.

"So," she began, captivating me with a word. "Big plans for the holiday?"

I stared, uncertain. "What holiday?"

"Halloween, of course." She grinned. "It's Saturday, or did you miss the bats, the cats, the witch boots, and the giant pumpkins strewn on every available surface?"

I chuckled, glancing around the coffee shop as if seeing the silly decorations for the first time. "Yes, of course. I just hadn't really thought much about the meaning behind them."

She hummed, taking a sip of her coffee, licking her top lip as she lowered the cup. I didn't think my poor cock could get much harder, but that flash of pink tongue managed to make that happen. Fuck, I was going to come for days when I finally got inside that mouth of hers.

"Perhaps you should put some thought to them. It's my favorite holiday, after all."

"Really?" I sat back, cocking my head, looking at her with new eyes.

"Of course. When else can we dress up to be who we really are?" She grinned, edging away from my table, the look in her eyes positively wicked. "Gotta run. See you tomorrow, new guy."

And with that, she was gone, out the door and striding toward what I assumed was her place of work. I waited, staring out the glass windows, watching her go. Licking my lips as her hips swung from side to side with each step. As her hair—loose and falling in waves halfway down her back today—danced in the breeze. She moved like sex, every inch of her body rolling in a rhythm as old as time. I wanted to feel that rhythm against me, wanted to know how tight those lips could wrap around my cock, how warm and wet I could get her before she surrendered to my ministrations. I wanted to taste the sweetness of her blood as I made her come.

When she turned the corner, I stood, palming my hard cock over my pants and moving it into a better position. Deplorable manners really, but necessary. Ignoring the blatant stares and surprised or possibly disgusted gasps of the patrons around me, I tossed my cup into the waste receptacle and stepped outside. Plum's honeyed death smell teased me, leading me in her direction. Making me grin.

The hunt had begun.

CHAPTER FIVE

Wednesday

WEDNESDAY MORNING, I AGAIN WAITED FOR MY Plum, taking the time to truly observe the Halloween decorations along the street. Pumpkins, both real and fake, added a bit of festivity to the otherwise dark buildings. Most of the so-called monsters seemed a bit tame, but every now and again, someone crossed that line from family-fun to scary. The werewolf with saliva dripping from his canines, his muzzle pulled back in what looked to be a loud snarl. The ghostly hands seeming to reach through a window at you, ready to steal you away from your reality into one of nightmares. And the vampire, fangs descended, blood dripping from the corner of his mouth. A little creepier, a little harsher. A little more honest.

I'd timed my arrival to meet Plum at the door,

eyeing her intently as I allowed her into the little storefront before me.

"Good morning, Plum," I murmured, leaning into her so my breath blew across her ear.

"Plum, huh? Interesting choice." She brushed against me as she passed. The way her cheeks curved and her pink lips tipped up in a smile confirmed that move was on purpose, making my mouth water and my neglected cock weep. "Good morning, new guy. Ready for Halloween yet?"

"Not quite yet. I think I need a bit more direction regarding the customs." I followed a little too closely as she weaved her way to the line of people waiting to order their morning motivation. Fuck politeness and appearances, I craved her scent. I sniffed, my eyes rolling at the sweetness, at the sugary depth to her smell, at the lingering aroma of death around her. Someone somewhere had made this woman for me. Of that, I had no doubt.

"Such as?"

I leaned over her, whispering into her ear. "Such as...what type of costume might someone like you be wearing come All Hallows' Eve?"

She turned, eyes bright. "I can't tell you that, new guy. It'd ruin the surprise."

At the counter, Plum ordered her regular coffee drink, but when it was time for her to pay, I stepped in.

"I've got this one," I said, keeping my voice low and firm, not giving her any room for an argument. She stared at me for a few seconds, not speaking. Finally, she blinked and nodded.

"Thank you," she whispered, stepping aside without a complaint. I liked that, liked knowing she'd do as I said with something as casual as my choosing to pay for her. I'd watched the people in this shop enough to know that was not something every person seemed willing to do. Most of these humans were set on showcasing their independence to the detriment of those attempting to be courteous. Most humans would never give up enough control to allow another to truly lead them. Plum was definitely not most humans.

I purposely brushed against her as I moved into her abandoned spot at the counter, copying her move from the doorway, wishing for skin-on-skin contact more than ever. "You're very welcome."

"And what can I get for you, sir?" the barista asked. I kept my attention on Plum, watching her expression harden as she took in the other woman. I appreciated the slight flare of jealousy, not that it was needed. My attention was for Plum alone.

"Espresso, please, and a croissant," I replied, offering the stranger barely a flicker of a glance. Instead, I leaned into Plum, again skimming her body with my arm as I looked over the glass case of pastries. Giving Plum a subtle smile as I nodded toward the various options. "Anything else for you?"

Plum smiled, looking slightly surprised. She swept her eyes over the case before that smile turned into something a little more sensual. "I'll have a scone. A plum and honey scone, please."

My mouth turned up in what had to be a wicked

grin, and my cock responded to the challenge in her eyes. Well played, Plum. Well played.

"Of course," the barista responded, having no idea what little power play my Plum had just pulled off. I paid quickly, keeping my focus on Plum, enjoying the hell out of her sensuous smirk.

"You enjoy plums?" I asked her as we moved to the side to wait for our order.

She shrugged, that smirk growing wider. "They grow on you."

I huffed a chuckle, a sound I hadn't made in many, many decades. "Yes, they certainly do."

We stood at the pickup station, our arms touching but otherwise looking like any other pair who happened to end up in the same space. Mostly. Because her scent teased me, the warmth of her body inviting me toward her. I followed that invitation. And Plum stayed right beside me, almost leaning into me. Something I noticed with a sense of satisfaction. The two of us attracted as if magnetized. Connected from shoulder to elbow.

When the woman behind the counter handed us our drinks and food, I passed the unopened bag to Plum.

"What's this?" she asked, holding up the bag.

"A croissant and a scone."

"Well, yes. But I thought one was for you."

I lifted a shoulder, holding her gaze. "I'm not hungry."

Her eyebrow went up, along with one side of her mouth. "Big dinner last night? Something tasty and...warm?"

I froze, my smile stuck. Something in her tone, in the way she asked that question, set off a bit of an alarm inside my head. She couldn't know I'd been hunting the night before or that I'd followed her scent to the hospital a few blocks over. Couldn't have any idea about the woman who'd walked out of the almost-hidden employee entrance at the exact best—or worst in her regards—time. Whose body had been too thin to get me hard, whose blood had barely satiated my thirst. I'd burned that woman like the rest of them, made sure there was nothing left behind at the scene just as I had with every meal. Plum couldn't know what I'd done.

"Pardon?" I asked, holding on to my worry with a firm mental grip.

"Just wondering," she said with a shrug as she led me toward the door. "A man like you should be hungry all the time. Or so I'd think."

I hummed, opening the door for her, shaking off the unwarranted wariness. "I suppose you're right. I'm not much of a breakfast eater, though."

"No?"

"No. I much prefer to eat at night." I followed her down the block, not really making the choice to do so, simply drawn to her spirit and her scent in a way that precluded any actual decision-making.

"Night eater, huh? That's not good for you." Plum looked both ways before crossing the street, something adorable and slightly unusual considering the other humans ignoring traffic and focusing on their phones.

"I seem to be getting on well so far."

"Yes, you do." She looked me over, a hunger in her

eyes that made a growl rumble through me. One I was unable to hold back. Plum's eyes widened for a second before darkening, her body edging closer. As if the sound attracted her.

"Plum," I started, unsure what to say next, completely knocked off-balance by this woman.

"Thanks for the coffee and breakfast," she said, her voice softer, lower, more sensual. That tone spoke to me, aroused me.

"Anytime," I replied, meaning it. I'd do anything for her at any time. I was completely hers... All she had to do was ask, and I'd give her the world. Something I was glad she didn't seem to realize just yet.

I walked with her across the street, all the way to the corner where the hospital she worked sat. I had no idea what she did in that gargantuan building, but I figured that's what left the scent of death under her skin. The thing that had first caught my attention and called me to her side.

"You work over here?" she asked, scanning the crowded sidewalk. Hiding her knowing smile behind her coffee as she took a sip. I kept my face still, my body language casual. She knew I'd walked with her for the company. I didn't need to confirm it.

"A few blocks back," I lied.

"Oh." She nodded, totally not believing me. "Then why'd you come all this way?"

Surrendering, or perhaps simply taking what I wanted, I stepped into her space. My body met hers, sending heat and desire soaring through me. Stoking the sexual tension between us. Bringing my hand to her face, I ran a finger down her cheek. Softly. Lightly. Unable to resist a single second longer.

"Because taking a walk with a beautiful woman seemed much more interesting than anything else I could have had to do this morning."

Her face lit up, a smile spreading across her lips. One that melted me. She bent her head into my touch, letting me feel more, resting her cheek in my palm. Before I could move, she stepped closer. Pressing her breasts against my chest, her hip skimming across my aching cock. Teasing me with the lushness of her body.

"You're a charmer, new guy."

I leaned down, sniffing, pulling that scent deep within my body to get me through the next few hours alone. "I try, Plum."

"You succeed." She pulled back, stepping away from me. "Have a great day, new guy. See you tomorrow."

"You have a lovely day as well." I watched as she turned and walked away, my eyes glued to her back. A plan formulating in my mind. She wouldn't be seeing me as soon as she thought.

CHAPTER SIX

―――――――――

Thursday

By Thursday evening, I was close to losing control as I waited at the little coffee shop for my Plum. I'd not met her that morning, having hidden in the shadows at the back of the storefront to watch her instead. I'd wanted to tease her, to make her crave my presence, but I seemed to accomplish the opposite. She'd appeared anxious that I wasn't there—eyeing the door repeatedly, glancing at her phone screen as if checking the time, fingering the tail of the paper cat on a table beside her as she waited for her turn.

But then she'd stilled, calmed perhaps. And that naughty smile had returned to her lips. That finger had disappeared into her mouth as she nibbled on the end. Trailing it down her chin and neck, fingers spread to tickle her collarbone. Captivating me.

Turning the tables and making me crave her even more than I already had been.

She'd flirted with the male barista, leaning across the counter, giving him a view of her cleavage as she'd smiled and giggled at his teasing. Even telling him she'd be back after her shift was over. I'd barely held in my hiss at that particular line. Were her words an invitation? Would he take what was mine before I acted? Though, why I should care almost bothered me more than imagining the act. The woman was ripe and sensual; I'd normally have enjoyed watching someone else make her quiver and scream. It wasn't as if the barista would take her blood, would suckle that long neck the way I intended to. And yet, I'd have snapped his neck if he'd laid a single finger on her precious skin.

The woman drove me mad. Her curves, her softness, the seductive scent of death that seemed to cling to her. The way just the thought of her made my cock weep and my fangs descend. I wanted her blood and her body, and I was getting tired of waiting. Especially at that moment, sitting in the coffee shop looking out the windows as the sun set over the tops of the buildings across the street after not touching her for more than a day.

Kicking myself mentally, I glared at the paper fucking bats dancing in the wind as another person who wasn't my Plum came dashing into the shop. I should have met her in the morning as was our usual, but I'd wanted to keep her guessing. I'd wanted to make her wait. Funny, that delay had driven me to distraction, not her…or so it seemed.

Seconds before I rampaged the coffee shop—how late did she fucking work?—the door opened and my Plum walked in, her hair a mess and her clothes rumpled. She looked tired, pale…and more beautiful than I'd ever seen her before. I kept my seat, dissolving into the shadows once more, my shoulders finally relaxing as my world righted itself. She'd arrived, her scent overpowering the brewed coffee aroma in the air. I still couldn't touch her, couldn't lean into her warm body and scent her neck, but I had a plan. I was going to learn more about her.

Plum ordered at the counter, leaning over the edge like on the first day we met. Her ass looked amazing in the tight, black breeches she wore. Curvy and full, enough for my hands to grab and squeeze without hurting her. Unless she wanted to be hurt. Unless she liked a little pain mixed with her pleasure. I certainly hoped she did.

Once she'd paid, Plum stepped to the side, standing a little taller, seeming a bit more awake. She glanced my way, and I could have sworn her eyes met mine for a moment—the briefest of seconds—but that wasn't possible. I'd dissolved enough to be something humans wouldn't see. They'd know someone was in my place, but I would be indistinct. More the impression of a person than the reality of one. Only other vampires could see through our disguises. No, there was no way she knew I was there… It had to be a sort of wishful thinking on my part.

My Plum walked out of the shop without looking around again, coffee in hand, eyes forward as she navigated the crowded sidewalk. I followed at a distance, not wanting to alarm her or alert her to my presence. She paused outside a store with a bright purple light shining over the window, that wicked smile back on her mouth. The one that gripped me, calling me to kiss it right off her pretty face. But I didn't...I held back, hiding among the shadows.

Once she'd continued on her way, I followed to where she'd paused. The window was decorated garishly like so many others, a bright, colorful Halloween scene depicted in paper forms and plastic ephemera. But what caught my eye was the large vampire hanging from the ceiling, looming over the other miscellany. Dark eyes, blood on his lips, fangs bared...he looked very scary. And much more true to form than most. Interesting.

Was that paper vampire what had attracted her attention? Did she have a fantasy about vampires? Many humans did, much to our chagrin. Or perhaps more of a fetish, aroused by the idea of our strong, almost alien nature. Nipples hard thinking about the way blood and sex could be brought together. Yes, interesting indeed.

Leaving the window behind, I stalked Plum the rest of the way down the street. My eyes locked on her ass. Fuck, I wanted to crawl inside her. The way her hips swayed, how strands of hair that had escaped her messy bun blew back in the wind, the scent of death drawing me closer. I wanted her. I needed to find out what her life entailed, when I could slip inside of it and take my fill. Because I didn't just want her blood. I wanted her mouth and her hand, I wanted her pussy. And I wouldn't stop until I had it all.

Two turns and three blocks later, she reached a small brownstone in a nondescript part of town. I dissolved into shadows across the street, waiting, watching as she entered the building. I needed to know, had to figure out which unit was hers. There was no way I could walk away from her just yet.

Five seconds…ten…and then lights blazed in the windows on the top floor.

"Gotcha," I whispered, dematerializing and sending myself up to the fire escape outside her window. Remaining in my shadow form, I watched as she moved about her apartment. Light and bright but bare, the place told me nothing about her. Not a hint, not a picture. Just beige walls and wood floors, ugly furniture and very little of it. My Plum was still a mystery.

But then she began to undress, and my thoughts left what was inside the room. My eyes stayed locked on her body as each piece of clothing fell to the floor. Her shirt and bra first, revealing heavy breasts with dark nipples, perfect for pinching or sucking. They swayed as she bent to remove her pants, long legs appearing from beneath the black cotton, tiny white panties covering the very best parts of her. The parts I'd been obsessed with since the first day.

Dark ink stood out against her pale skin. A triangle with a flame on one side, the entire thing made up of knotted lines and thick strands woven together. Small, in a spot on her shoulder blade easily concealed by most clothing, the image piqued my curiosity but baffled my memory. One I'd seen before but didn't recognize. Something I couldn't concentrate on as her body moved and twisted, as she stood almost naked before me.

Unable to resist, I solidified once more, pulling the shadows to me to stay relatively hidden from any passerby. I unzipped my pants and pulled my cock through the opening, nearly shaking in my need. Fingers wrapping around my length, I stroked from base to tip. Thumb rubbing over the head on one pass, twisting a bit on the next. Fuck, it felt good. Not as good as I knew my Plum would feel around me, though. She'd be tight and wet, warm and silky as I slid inside.

When she moved into the bathroom, I edged across the fire escape, still stroking, still focused completely on her. Her bathroom window was neither frosted nor covered, giving me unadulterated access to her as she bent to turn on the taps. Steam billowed from the tub. My Plum wiggled her way out of her panties, dropping the cotton to the floor and leaving me with an unobstructed view of her ink, of her ass. Perfect and round, it was made to be smacked. To be bitten. To be worshiped.

She turned, raising her arms to release the messy bun. Her breasts lifted, and the dark, trimmed patch of hair at the apex of her legs screamed woman. Fuck, I moved my hand faster, craving her, needing to find my release before she hid her body behind the dark shower curtain.

Pulling, tugging, twisting, growling, I watched as she prepared for her shower, dying a little bit inside with every pass of my hand. But when she lifted her leg to step over the tub rim, when she gave me a glimpse of the sweet pink lips hidden in her most private spot, I fell. Grunting, I came in my free hand, pumping myself with the other to push that pleasure as far as I could. Hips thrusting into my fist.

Drained, not nearly satisfied, I bit my lip and leaned toward her bathroom window. Wiping my seed along the pane. Let another try to come for my Plum, my scent was on her home now. Marked. She was mine, and I'd kill anyone who tried to take her from me.

Before I could be distracted by thoughts of her naked body so close to me, I dissolved and took flight. Heading for my nest. Seeking a place to research that tattoo and perhaps replay every moment I'd seen from the fire escape again. Over and over. Cock hard and a hiss ready to leave my lips, I took off.

Knowing damn well I'd be back soon.

CHAPTER SEVEN

Friday

FRIDAY MORNING, I OPENED THE DOOR TO THE coffee shop for my Plum.

"A girl could get used to this." Her sassy grin made me smile, but her scent made me growl. I leaned into her, loving the way her breath caught and her pupils went wide.

"I certainly hope so."

I secured our beverages—latte for her, espresso for me—and another treat from the pastry case. Something a little different this time. I needed to keep her guessing.

When I handed her the bag, she grinned.

"What is it today?"

"Butterscotch bar. It sounds delightfully sweet."

She moaned, opening the bag and taking a sniff. "I love butterscotch."

"Then I chose correctly."

"Just don't start calling me that," she said, a glare so fake sitting on her pretty face I nearly laughed.

"Wouldn't dream of it, Plum." I indicated for her to lead the way, adjusting my cock as soon as she turned her back to me. Fuck, I could stare at her ass for days and never get enough.

We walked outside together, her heading toward work, me following along like a puppy on a leash. An irritating fact but one I refused to delve into. Until she was mine, I'd pretend to be tamed. Hell, I'd hump her leg if she'd let me.

"My stop," she said when we reached the corner near the hospital.

"Yes, I guess it is." I was beginning to hate the interruption her job represented, despise how she hid away in that building for so many hours of the day. Still, I sighed and did my best not to show my frustration. The smile she gave me held secrets and knowledge, as if she knew how desperate I was becoming. As if she felt the same.

"Perhaps I'll see you later."

I brushed my fingers across the back of her hand, pretending to direct her to the crosswalk, really just taking advantage of a chance to touch her. "I'm sure you will."

"Have a good day, new guy."

I took a step back, fighting back the need to grab her and run. To steal her away from her everyday life and drag her to my nest. To my bed.

Not yet…soon, but not yet.

"You too, Plum."

———

That night, I once again opened the coffee shop door for Plum, surprising her.

"What are you doing here so late?" she asked.

"I told you, I'm a night eater."

She laughed, stepping to the counter. Before I could order for her, she grabbed my arm, stopping me. That single touch, that simple move showing her comfort and familiarity with me, had my cock hardening in a painful way. This woman was going to kill me, certainly a difficult task seeing as I'd technically been dead for six centuries.

"Iced chai tea, please." Plum squeezed my arm before letting go. My cock twitched in response. Fuck, but I wanted to feel her hand wrapped around me, wanted to know how warm and soft she'd be…or how hard she'd work me over. I had a feeling my Plum wouldn't go easy on me, and I couldn't wait to find out for sure.

Distracting myself from the need to drag her into the restroom and fuck her against the wall, I cleared my throat. "That's not your usual."

She didn't shrug or look away. She stared right into my eyes, her gaze steady. Her expression one that said so many dirty things as she spoke mundane words laced with innuendo. "I like sweet things on my tongue at night."

A growl rumbling through my chest, I leaned over her body. Bringing us together. Touching her. My hand sliding to her hip to hold her still. Fuck, she smelled

good. My mouth watered as the thought of tasting her
—her skin, her blood, the sweetness of her pussy—ran
through my mind.

"So do I, Plum."

Her measured stare held mine, her lips turning up
in a wicked smirk. "Good to know."

Two beats, three, and then she looked away. Unable
to resist, I patted her ass as I motioned for the door. So
soft, so perfect for spanking.

Drinks in hand, we walked outside and down the
street. Quiet. Heading away from the hospital. Our
arms brushed as we swayed, our fingers staying close
together. Affection wasn't something I was accustomed
to, but I wanted to experience it with Plum. I wanted to
hold her, hug her, do simple things like clasp her hand
in mine. That didn't belie the fact that I wanted to
thrust my cock deep inside her and make her scream my
name, it merely added to the draw. Increased the
tension and made me crave her all that much more. An
interesting and unusual phenomena for sure.

"I'll be sad when all the Halloween decorations are
gone next week," Plum said as we passed my favorite
paper vampire in a window display.

"Why?" I asked, truly curious. The purple light
shining from the display created a strange, monstrous
halo effect around her. Turning her into some kind of
perverse angel.

"It's my favorite holiday."

"Don't most hu—" I paused, coughed, redirecting
my words "—people enjoy the Christmas season more?"

Plum smirked, turning to continue our walk

through the dead leaves and decoration debris piling up. "Perhaps, but I prefer Halloween. Where I'm from, we celebrate the entire week leading up to the All Hallows' feast. Tonight, for example, would be Devil's Night. The night the demons come out to play."

I nodded, following her as she turned down her street. "And what would those demons do to the poor, unsuspecting humans?"

She spun, facing me as she walked backward, grinning. "Anything those poor humans wanted them to."

"Naughty demons," I replied, humored by her obvious excitement.

"Damn right." She spun back around, walking by my side, close enough to keep our arms touching.

Passing a townhome just off the main drag, the unmistakable scent of vampire danced on the air. Someone close. Someone I didn't know or recognize, who probably wouldn't comprehend the danger of getting too close to the Master's own sired son. I held back a growl, fighting to remain humanesque so as not to scare my Plum. Still, someone was close…someone who might scent another vampire around an unclaimed human and decide to take her for himself. That couldn't happen.

Plum walked and sipped her tea, unaware of the rage and terror building within me. I was ready to defend her, ready to kill any threat to her. Eyes open, scanning the street for any sign of one of my kind, I followed her all the way home.

"This is me," she said as we reached her building.

I glanced up the façade, scanning the balconies, knowing I'd need to access the roof as soon as Plum was safely inside. "Yes, I suppose it is."

"You suppose?"

The teasing tone of her voice dragged my attention back to her, the threat of another vampire in the area temporarily put on hold as I backtracked over what I'd said.

"I have to assume," I said, lifting one shoulder in a casual sort of way. "It's not as if I've been inside your apartment before."

"Hmmm, inside." That wicked smirk returned, that knowing look in her eyes a tease and a promise. "No, you haven't been inside, have you?"

My growl was uncontrollable, my hand grabbing her hip and pulling her to me something I had no power to stop. "You shouldn't tease me."

"Oh, new guy. I'm definitely not teasing." She ran a finger down my neck, making me shiver. Making me quake with an absolute need to devour her. "Though I am tired tonight."

I leaned into her touch, resting my cheek against hers as I whispered, "Plus you have demons to play with."

Her lips touched my skin, a soft brush, just enough to make me grasp her harder. Pull her tighter. To make my cock ache with the need to be inside her.

"Maybe I'm the demon doing the playing."

"Naughty demon."

She grinned. "Damn right."

I laughed, backing away, knowing I needed to

investigate her building before I could settle in to watch her for the night. "Goodnight, Plum."

She smiled, those dark eyes lit with something fiery and needful. Something that stoked the flames within me.

"See you soon, new guy."

As she hurried through the door, I waited, watching. Making sure she was safely upstairs before moving. As soon as I crept into the deeper shadows, I dissolved, streaking up to the top of her building. Breathing deeply, I scented the air. Nothing. No trace of vampire, no energy of the undead around. Not that I truly expected there to be. Vampires were much more prevalent in the city than any human could possibly consider. I ran across ones I'd never met multiple times a week. But this one was close to my Plum. She was mine, and I wouldn't allow anything to take her from me. No matter what.

Once I'd paced the roofline, spitting every few feet to clearly mark this place as under my guard, I dissolved once again and headed for Plum's fire escape. I was on edge, needing to know she was safe, but also craving a release. Craving her body and her touch. Our little moments had been nothing but a tease, a prelude to something bigger. Something more. And I wanted to get to that main event.

Plum was in her bedroom, lying across her mattress in the dark. But she definitely wasn't sleeping. Her clothes were strewn across the room, her panties hooked around one ankle. Supporting herself on her knees and elbows, head down, ass facing the window. One hand buried between her legs. Fingers inside herself. Plunging, gripping, pressing, sliding, grinding…fucking.

I stared, transfixed. Sounds of sex—of wet skin coming together, of heavy breaths and tiny moans— kissed my ears, drawing me closer. My nose pressing against cold glass as my eyes stayed locked on the vision before me. Watching her fingers disappear inside herself, licking my lips as her legs tensed and foot flexed, almost whimpering as her hips rocked back against her hand. Fucking hell.

I grabbed my cock through my pants as her fingers dipped deeper into that swollen, pink flesh. Fuck, I wanted to be inside with her. I wanted to feel her, taste her, watch her come. I wanted to be causing that frenzy, that sheen spreading down her thighs, that flush on the cheeks of her round ass.

Obviously frustrated, she spread her knees wider, leaning her upper body on one shoulder and bringing that hand to her clit. I couldn't move fast enough, couldn't free my cock from the confines of my trousers in time for the sight before me. Couldn't waste a single second more. I'd never in all my years been so jealous of someone else's hands.

As she rode her fingers toward orgasm, I worked my cock. Hard, rough strokes, yanking at a furious pace. Needing to match her rhythm. Pretending it was her pussy wrapped around me. Though I knew—I was absolutely certain—her pussy would be a thousand times better than my hand. Softer, warmer, and so fucking wet for me. I'd make her drip before the night was over, make her feel the need to wipe the wetness from her thighs. It was a mission I was absolutely going to succeed at.

Just before I came, right as my balls tightened, Plum rocked back, pushing three fingers deep, groaning out something that sounded like a word. That sounded like a curse. I came hard, spattering along her windowsill. Marking this place as mine once more. Making sure the other vamp on the block understood he'd be dealing with me should he dare to even look at my Plum. Soon, I'd need to bite her, to make sure her body smelled of mine. To protect her.

But not tonight. Even with the tingles of my orgasm still racing up my spine, I knew I was too far over the limit of my control to be with her. If I tried to get near her tonight, I'd fuck her through the floor and drain her dry. I needed to take the edge off first.

I needed to hunt again.

CHAPTER EIGHT

Saturday Morning

On the morning of Halloween, Plum didn't show up at the coffee house. I waited for close to an hour, claws puncturing the fake-leather couch I sat upon. With every minute, every human walking through the door who was not my Plum, the fiery rage within me burned brighter and hotter until I couldn't take another second. I rushed out the door. Headed for her apartment, dissolving into shadow without thought to those around me. While the sun didn't burn us alive as modern pop culture suggested, it made our shadow-walking next to impossible. We were creatures of the night, made of darkness, so we tended to keep nocturnal hours to avoid the daylight. Traveling in our preferred manner when it was bright and sunny made for a difficult journey. But for my Plum, I would do anything.

Plum was still asleep when I made it to her window, all dark hair and white bedding, one long leg casually thrown on top of the blankets as if she'd grown warm. Desperate to make sure she was all right, to touch her skin and calm the madness within, I dissolved and rematerialized inside her apartment.

With my first breath, I knew I'd made a mistake.

Her scent permeated the room, concentrated in such a small space, making my mouth water and my cock throb. Sweat, death, and sex hung heavy in the air, proof of the orgasm she'd had the night before as I'd watched. As I died my own little death to the sight of her fingers deep inside her pussy. Fuck, the need to own her grew stronger every day, every hour. I wouldn't last much longer without my cock in her pussy and my teeth in her flesh.

I took another breath, this one deeper, trying to devour her essence in any way I could. The sticky sweetness of plums in the air tantalized me. As if she'd bathed with the flesh, as if she were covered in syrupy juice. The scent drew me closer, stole what was left of my control. Too far gone to worry about consequences, I crept to the edge of her bed, knees brushing the white comforter casually tossed over her body. Her skin called to me, made me crave her, made me shake with my need to feel her. I slipped one hand down to stroke my cock over my trousers, wanting to calm the ache. I let the other drop to her knee, floating over her skin for ten seconds…fifteen…until I couldn't resist any longer.

Barely touching her—a single finger circling her knee, edging up her thigh—I gave in to my desires. A simple brush of her flesh, a tiny touch that could soothe the deep ache within. That was it…all I needed. I could regain my control, could leave her to her slumber knowing she was safe. I could—

Plum rolled over, the comforter twisting almost all the way off, her legs falling open. Pink flesh normally hidden, revealed against a sea of white cotton, a tiny patch of dark curls drawing my eyes. Calling to me. Begging me to touch, to taste. To spread her open and discover every secret nook, every spot that made her gasp. To make her shake with desire.

To take what I so desperately wanted.

Unable to resist, I allowed my finger to continue its trek, tracing the path of her femoral artery, up her thigh to the secret place that so intrigued me. Hovering over the warm flesh, lightly tickling the curls I wanted to bury my face in. A single swipe along the lush softness of her lips. No more. Though, I didn't pull my hand away, too enticed by her warmth to give up. Too obsessed with her pussy to stop touching, staring, craving.

Plum groaned as her blood began to pool under my fingers. Swelling her flesh. Making her wet for me, warm. Aroused. I wanted to taste her, to feel her on my tongue, to fuck her hard with my hand, to drink from that spot where her leg joined into her hip. That magical sweet spot that would taste like blood and sex and Plum. I wanted to send her into orgasm with little more than my mouth and drink down every drop of her pleasure.

I wanted to bury my cock inside of her far more than I wanted to drink her blood.

Before I could force that thought to make sense, her phone rang. Cursing the shrill sound, I dissolved without thought, reappearing in the darkness of her closet. Back in the shadows where I belonged but still surrounded by Plum's scent.

"Hello?" she mumbled, half-asleep, curling herself back under her blankets, much to my dismay. "Hey. No, I don't work today or tomorrow. It's my first weekend off in months."

She groaned and rolled a bit, toes flexing as she listened, the words coming from the other end of the conversation too tinny for me to understand.

"Not yet. Soon, though. I can't see it taking much longer." A pause. Plum bent her leg at the knee, letting the comforter drop, her fingers running in a pattern along her thigh. Along the exact same path mine had only moments before. I leaned against the doorframe, hard and aching for her, watching her through the slit she'd left open. Fuck, what I wouldn't give to walk back into her bedroom and throw that comforter off her body. I'd push her knees down to the mattress, spread her wide, and devour her. Make her come before she could even hang up the phone. Give the person on the other end something interesting to listen to.

Plum hummed, dropping her knee, letting her hand fall slack along her hip. Her fingers brushing the curls between her legs. "Yeah, sounds good. I'll meet you at the Carnival at ten. Okay. See you tonight."

She rolled to her back, tossing an arm over her face.

Almost immediately, her breathing deepened, her heart rate dropping to a slow and even pace. Back asleep, though this time almost completely covered by her blankets. I wanted to stay, to watch her sleep and sneak into her bed. To wake her with my body on top of hers. But I would resist that urge and leave her for the afternoon.

Besides, I knew she'd be leaving by ten. And I was enough of a bastard to want to know exactly who she'd agreed to go to the Carnival with. Every vampire in the state knew that club. It was a warehouse of sin, filled to the brim with humans ready to do almost anything. Woven through the throngs, attracted by the sweat and the blood and the sex, all sorts of creatures of the night hunted. The Carnival was a buffet of human flesh that my kind—and more—took full advantage of.

No one would be taking advantage of my Plum tonight, though.

I dematerialized and rushed out the window, heading for my nest. There were preparations to be made and favors to be called in. Plum would be heading to the Carnival with friends, but she'd be leaving with me. Not before I bit her, though. Claimed her right there in the middle of a vampire feeding ground.

I'd make sure they all knew she belonged to the Master's son.

CHAPTER NINE

Saturday Night

WITH A NOD TO THE BODYGUARD AT THE DOOR—
the son of a demon, if I remembered correctly—I
walked into the Carnival unheeded, following a safe
distance behind my prey. The music was loud, the lights
strategically low on the fringes, and the dance floor was
packed. All distractions I couldn't afford. I kept an eye
on my Plum, watching her ass sway in her short skirt,
the muscles in her long legs as she worked her way
through the crowd, the shimmer of her back exposed by
the draping of her blood-red top. She'd strolled in with
two other women, all of them looking like sex…like sin.
Looking like women who knew exactly what they
wanted and how to get it.

The club was crowded, jam-packed with humans in
an array of costumes, out to enjoy Halloween. The
heady combination of sweat and heat in the air set my

instincts ablaze, making me hard, horny, and hungry in mere seconds. The whole place was one big pit of heartbeats and sex, right at the edge of something, a giant orgasm ready to happen. That energy, that thrill, fed my own needs. Made me desire Plum more, made me long for her. But that would stop tonight, because soon, I'd have her.

I followed Plum to the dance floor where she and her friends found an opening and took over the space. They danced closely, bodies pressed together at times, attracting attention but ignoring most of it. At least Plum did. Arms up, hips swaying, they moved to the music in a sensual rhythm impossible to deny. Enticing their prey with their beauty and sexuality. I watched the show from the sidelines, a smirk growing across my face. These girls knew exactly what they were doing, and they were good at it. They could have just about any man in this club at their beck and call, but instead, they focused on each other. Laughing, talking, rubbing up against one another when the mood hit them. A beautiful tease of a treat indeed.

But I still only wanted Plum.

"I see you took my advice." Samuelson appeared beside me, staring out over the crowd.

"I'm not here to hunt." I stayed my ground, eyes locked on Plum.

"Ah, found what you've been looking for then?" He laughed, nodding his head toward the dance floor. Toward my Plum. "I see you've become taken with the necromancers. Which one of the three has captured your interest?"

"Necromancers? What are you talking about?" My cock twitched at the thought. Death speakers...links between the living and the not. Necromancers were very much the wet dream of the vampire world. They tended to ensnare us, to attract us. And we definitely attracted them. But unlike mediums, who merely talked to the dead, necromancers could also traverse planes of existence, making them exceedingly rare. I'd met one in the past century, but a coupling with her hadn't worked out. To have three in the same area, actually spending time together, was unheard of. No wonder the Carnival had been so busy lately. Every vamp in the state would be flocking to the area to get a look, attempt to get a taste.

Samuelson grinned when he saw what had to be my gobsmacked expression, his canines descended too far to pass for human teeth. "You don't know, do you? Those three ladies dance with death on a regular basis. They also know what we are without having to tell them. They feel the death within us."

I stared at Plum, mouth agape. She knew. Had known from the start. And still, she let me touch her, let me be near her. She didn't run from me.

"Necromancers." I shook my head, unable to believe my good fortune. I'd somehow stumbled on to a woman who could talk to the dead. Who understood it, courted it even. No wonder I'd become obsessed with her. She smelled like death because she dealt with it, and not just in her job. Her entire life was death.

"They'd make good donors. No fear to taint the blood, no need to thrall them into a submissive state."

Samuelson crossed his arms over his chest and leaned back against the rail behind us. "Though you might not want to delay, old friend. I think Brannon has caught the scent of them himself."

My eyes darted from shadow to shadow until I spotted the vampire in the darkest corner. Brannon was the son of Bran, another one of Master's closest allies. I'd never met him officially, but I didn't doubt he was behind the vamp scent on Plum's block. He looked hungry in a way that spoke of a deep need, of a wanting I understood. He'd been close to Plum, maybe all three of the girls, probably watching them as I had Plum. Craving their blood and their bodies. He was hunting, but that would end tonight.

Brannon and Samuelson would be an even match on the social status of our race, though I would still sit a notch above. That fact fueled my desire to claim Plum immediately. Even with the respect a vampire like Samuelson or Brannon offered me, they wouldn't wait forever. They'd jump in and take her from me if I didn't act.

As Brannon took a step out of the dark, his red hair reflecting the lights shining down from the rigging at the ceiling, Samuelson laughed.

"I do believe your time is up, old friend."

I hissed under my breath, my fangs descending at the possibility of a fight. "Yes, I think you're right."

"Best of luck to you." Samuelson took a step forward, matching mine. "I think I might try to charm an evening out of one of the others. Seeing as how you need to separate your prey from the herd."

I nodded once. "Tall, long hair, red top. The other two matter not."

Brannon moved toward the floor, eyes dancing from the girls to us and back. Wary. Wanting to claim but not wanting to battle, I assumed. He didn't charge, didn't try to cut me off. He stepped carefully, giving me the respect I deserved, which worked in his favor.

A little nudge from my thrall and Plum's friends slowly lost their focus, becoming distracted by others around them. The blonde was lured to the side of the dance floor, only to meet up with Samuelson as he edged her way. The shorter brunette spun right into Brannon's arms. The vamp sent me a single head nod in response, knowing exactly what I'd done. The gift I'd placed in his hands.

The two girls otherwise occupied left my Plum dancing alone in the middle of the floor, just as I planned. All I cared about, all I wanted, was her. Blood, body, mind…every bit. And I wanted her to myself…mostly.

I slipped across the floor, the crowd parting for me, my full attention on the woman in the blood-red top. Fitting, really, considering how badly I wanted to tear into her flesh and drink her down. But not yet. First, I was going to taste another part of her. The lovely pink skin that'd been playing on repeat through my memories all day. I wanted to tease her, feel those tightly wound curls tickle my lips. I wanted to fuck her with my tongue in front of everyone, let them know who owned her pussy. Because I did, or at least I would once I officially claimed her. And I'd do it in the club, making sure every vampire knew my little necromancer was officially unavailable to them.

Plum turned as I reached her, catching my eye, her face aglow in the pulsing lights. And then she smiled. Bright red lips curving up into a delicious arc that had me quickening my step. She continued to dance, eyes falling closed, hands running down the length of her body. Teasing me. Inviting me.

I moved beside her, lightly touching her arm, lining up our bodies before I leaned down to whisper in her ear.

"Do you come here often?"

Her head fell back as she laughed, mouth open, teeth practically glowing white against her red lips. The sound carried over the music, loud and bright. Attracting other men's attention. Capturing mine.

"Pretty sure I've heard that before, new guy."

I leaned into her, pulling her scent into my lungs. "It seemed to work relatively well the last time I tried it."

"Yeah, I guess it did." She inched closer, pressing her breasts to my chest. Inviting me.

I slid an arm around her waist, pulling her hips flush to mine. Trapping my half-hard cock between us. Knowing she felt it, that she'd feel it grow as her body writhed against me. Liking that she didn't pull away from me as the evidence of my desire for her lengthened. It took a few seconds, barely a full line from the chorus of the current song, before I was fully hard. Plum stared into my eyes and worked her body in a way to continuously rub against me. Teasing. Arousing further. Fuck, the woman would unman me in the middle of the dance floor if I let her.

"I didn't know vampires danced," Plum said, watching me, a slight tilt to her lips.

I shook my head, still slightly amazed at my luck. "This one doesn't usually."

"Why now?"

I pulled her tighter, grinding against her. "How could I resist the company?"

"Such a charmer."

"I do try, Plum."

We danced together like that for two songs, moving to the rhythm around us, slowly inching even closer, teasing with light touches and small rubs. Keeping our hips pressed tight. Arm around her waist, I inched my hand lower, my fingers resting against her ass. When she didn't balk, I went further, gripping her ass with one hand. Squeezing as her eyes fluttered closed and she sighed. Fuck, did her flesh in my hand feel good. All soft and full, made for pinching, biting, smacking, spanking. Made for a creative man such as myself.

The weight of other men's stares stoked the fire within me, my beastly side making its presence known. Those looks, the leers, left me wanting to glower, to grab her, to prove my ownership. So I spun her, drawing her into my arms, her back tight against my chest. I glared over her shoulder, focusing on one man who couldn't seem to understand that Plum was mine. His stare was more intense than the rest, more covetous in nature. His was the one I hated the most.

Eyes on his, I slid my hand down the front of Plum's

body, along the side of her breast, spreading my fingers across her stomach. He licked his lips as her hips ground against me, eyes nearly black with lust. More so than a human, not at all like a vampire. Some sort of demon perhaps. Whatever his kind, he would not be getting close to my Plum.

Instead of snapping his neck and draining him dry, I slid my hand lower, under Plum's skirt, fingers dancing beneath the silky panties she wore. Skin on skin, her body arching into my touch, her hands up around my neck. He watched, swallowed hard, the scent of desire wafting from him. I waited, ready. Finally, he glanced up and met my glare. Saw the monster waiting to jump out of me. I didn't hold back, letting my eyes go fully black, curling my upper lip into a snarl so he could see my fangs. The power the Master had given me fully on display. His desire quickly morphed to fear, making me hiss. His weakness a tease for the predator within. Without another look, he turned and disappeared into the crowds. Giving up. Submitting to my beast as I'd expected him to. Demon or not, there wasn't much that could or would fight a vampire. Not voluntarily, at least.

Still, his being there had gotten my hand close to Plum's pussy, something I hadn't expected. Dancing in the middle of the floor with my hand inside her panties…people watching, seeing, knowing what I was doing to her. Fantasizing they were in her spot or mine. Such a seductive scene. I wasn't about to miss this chance.

"All these men want you," I whispered in her ear, pulling her tighter, working my fingers lower, into the patch of curls between her legs. "They see you dancing, see us together, and they think of sex."

"Good." Her hips thrust forward, forcing my hand lower, my fingers finding her hidden, wet flesh.

"Good?" I ran my lips down her jaw, my fangs along her throat, teasing her, keeping my hand still as she moved against it. "Why is that good?"

"Because that's the goal tonight. That's what I want."

"You want sex? With a stranger?" I yanked her closer, let my fingers slide over her clit, pressed my cock against her ass. So hard, so needy. So fucking ready to dive inside her.

"No, not a stranger." Her eyes met mine, dark and pupils wide. "Someone I know."

I kept a tight hold on my thrall, not wanting to influence her, wanting her to want me. That level of desire, the arousal, sweetened the blood. Made the meal that much more enjoyable. Plus I wanted to see what this woman had in mind.

"It's Halloween, new guy. A time to celebrate the opening of the doors between realms. When monsters walk the earth disguised as humans." She leaned her head on my shoulder, looking up at me. "When your kind gets to come out and play."

"Naughty girl, Plum, knowing what I was and hiding that from me."

"I liked watching you decide which you wanted more, vampire. My blood or my body." She dropped a hand between us, running up the length of my cock in one rough stroke. "What did you decide?"

I yanked her back against my chest again, letting my fingers work their way deeper. Circling her clit once, twice, ten times before reaching to find where she was wet and swollen. Soft and warm. I slid my fingers inside as Plum pushed against me, her head thrown back. Her eyes closing as I worked my fingers in and out, teasing her, making her shake. Once my fingers slipped easily inside of her, I brought them back to her clit. Rubbing it. Squeezing. Pressing as I rocked her ass against my cock.

All the while, we continued to dance, hidden in plain sight within the crush of bodies on the dance floor. My fingers inside her, my cock pressed against her ass. Grinding and thrusting and teasing her toward her breaking point. Knowing others were watching. Loving the feeling of their eyes on me, on Plum, on the two of us.

"Both. I want your blood and body. Together. Now."

As her body heated, the scent of her arousal joined the mix of sex and blood and sweat of the club. Hot and heady, it overpowered me, making me pull her a little too hard, thrust inside her a little too fast. Still, she took it all, keeping her arms around my neck. Pulling me to curve around her. Wanting more.

"What's your name, new guy?" she asked, her voice breathy. A sound that made my cock practically weep.

"I'm Masterson."

"The vampire Master's sired son has his hands in my panties? I feel as if I just won a prize."

The fact that she knew naming customs of my

people should have surprised me, but it didn't. Nothing about my Plum surprised me anymore. Nothing mattered, either, except what was about to happen. What we'd been dancing around for days.

Leaning over her body, fingers moving fast and hard between her legs, I sucked on her earlobe. Once, twice, biting lightly. Letting my fangs grow long and sharp. Making her gasp when I broke the skin. A tiny little tease for me. She didn't pull away, so I didn't stop. Instead, I drew the bit of flesh into my mouth, lapping up the sweet, tantalizing blood dripping from the wound. My taste buds exploded, the sweetness almost too much, nearly cloying, but yet not. Tempered by something darker. Deeper. More like the smell of death around her, that air of the necromancer. Fucking amazing.

"You're so delicious, Plum. Your skin, your sweat, your blood…perfection. I can't wait until I bury my face in your pussy. I want to taste you come."

She whimpered, spreading her legs, one arm dropping to press on the back of my hand as if needing more. I didn't blame her; I needed more, as well. Growling loud and long as I pressed my hard cock against her ass and ground into her, I looked around the club, ignoring the human patrons staring at the two of us. Glaring hard at the vamps and not-quite humans to let them know to keep their distance. I needed a place to take her. I could thrall the whole club, make the two of us invisible, and fuck Plum in the middle of the dance floor, but the non-humans would still see us. They'd watch her come undone. No, that wouldn't do. I wanted the illusion of fucking her in front of a crowd, but I didn't want to share her face or her body, didn't want anyone else to know that part of her. So we'd need a bit of privacy for what I wanted to do to her.

Plum jerked, gasping, pressing harder against my cock. Fuck, she was close. In a crowd of people, in the middle of a dance floor with music blasting and bodies all around us, she was right on the edge. Head back, eyes closed, my body wrapped around hers, ready to come, to fall, to feel that rush. I wasn't far behind her.

Releasing her ear, I nuzzled into her neck, running my teeth along the length. My fingers slid through her wetness growing between her thighs, brushing her soaked curls. A dream, that's what Plum was. Gorgeous, sexy, willing, adventurous, and with a body that responded to my smallest touch. But I couldn't drink from her, not more than my little taste at her ear, not yet. I licked the length of her neck, buried my fingers deep inside her and pressed on her clit. She went stiff, so close. Wanting more, needing to get her alone, I stilled and placed my mouth next to her ear.

"Shall we go someplace we can…talk?"

She whimpered, tried to move against me, to ride my hand. "Masterson."

"Let me take you somewhere, Plum." I nibbled along her neck, almost desperate. I wanted to fuck her and bite her, wanted my cock covered in the wetness from her pussy and my chin covered in her blood. I wanted to devour every fucking inch of her. "Come on, beautiful. We'll find a spot so I can continue, some dark corner where I can make you beg for it."

I slid my fingers out, ran them along the length of her, and gave her clit a squeeze. She jerked, her body going tight. She was so close, so ready to quake around me. Completely on edge and at my mercy, but not because of my thrall. Not because of anything I'd forced her to do. She was ready because she liked what I was doing, was willing to let me continue. And that was a huge fucking turn-on.

"Okay," she said, quiet but strong. Reluctantly pulling my fingers from her panties, I surveyed the bar once more. Looking for shadows, for a spot I could take her. When I found it, I spun her around to face me. And then I froze. Face flushed, eyes wide, pupils somewhat blown...she was the epitome of aroused. Ready. Shaking with her need to come. Fucking perfect. I smiled and held her gaze as I brought my hand to my mouth, the one I'd been fucking her with. The one covered in her. As she watched, I licked the length of my fingers, tasting her, sucking her from my skin. My eyes nearly rolling back in my head as I hummed my appreciation.

"Delicious, Plum. Just as I knew you'd be."

"Fuck, Masterson."

"That's the plan." I grabbed her hand and tugged her behind me, letting my thrall clear a path, dragging her to a dark spot under a set of open, metal stairs. The shadows were deeper here, and the high tables with dark netting draped across them would hide much of what I was about to do to her from any non-human who chose to watch. I usually liked the idea of people around us, of glances our way as I owned her body. But aspects of this would be mine and mine alone. I would never share my Plum.

"Hold tight to the top, my sweet." I edged between her and the table, her arms on either side of me.

"Why?" she asked, all breathy and wide-eyed. "What are you going to do?"

"I'm going to make you come on my tongue, sweet. And then I'm going to fuck you. Hands on the table. Don't make me tell you again." I placed her hands on the tabletop and ducked underneath, dissolving just enough to keep from being seen. Shoving her skirt up her hips and ripping the panties off her, I dove into her pussy like a man possessed. Demanding a taste and taking what was so freely offered. Grabbing her leg, lifting her thigh onto my shoulder, I made her shiver and shake with my ministrations. Made her groan as I used my mouth on her. Long licks with my tongue, teeth and lips playing with her clit, sucking every drop of her down. Feasting on her.

Plum shivered and shook as I suckled her clit hard, as I slid two fingers inside. As I purred against her. Gasping, clinging to the table, rolling her hips against my face, she worked for every bit of her pleasure. And I loved that. Loved that she wasn't afraid to take what she wanted right there. No fear of people seeing, no care to what others thought. Plum was out to get exactly what she wanted, the rest of the club be damned.

In the middle of a flat-tongued lick that had Plum's knees shaking, a waitress approached the table. I heard her before I felt her, felt her before she was too close to see what was going on. Plum froze, body stiff, not pulling away but not moving, either. I grinned and gave her clit a nip, making her jump just as the waitress reached the table. This would be fun.

"Can I get you anything?" she asked my Plum, who had both hands holding on to the tabletop as if her life depended on it. Instead of going easy on her, giving her a break in front of the other woman, I thrust my fingers deeper, suckling her clit. Refusing to give her a single inch.

"Ah…no. I…no, thanks."

I gripped Plum's hips, pulling her to me, purring against her flesh, making her shiver. Backing away for a second, releasing her clit, I gave Plum a moment to relax. Then I ran my free hand up between her legs. I teased her with my thumb, getting it good and wet as I kept fucking her with my other hand, then trailed it back. Farther still. Pressing my thumb between her ass cheeks.

"You sure?" the waitress asked, making me chuckle. Poor Plum. I pressed my thumb into her little hole, slowly working the tip inside. Plum's knees shook, her body wound tight, ready to explode.

"Yeah…yes. I'm sure. Positive. I want… nothing…from you."

I purred louder, making sure she felt it as the waitress walked away. Plum's body sagged, her hands relaxing their grip on the table. But not for long. I pushed my thumb inside her ass, teasing her as I added a third finger to her pussy. As I licked a long, wide swath across her clit.

"Fuck, Masterson," she groaned, inching her legs apart, giving me more room.

Sticky sweetness coated my mouth and chin, making me purr louder. Plum gasped when she felt the vibration against her sensitive flesh, nearly stumbling in her efforts to press herself closer. Grabbing her hips, holding her still, I pressed my mouth against her and did it again, making the sound more animal, my fingers and thumb moving faster. Harder. Giving more.

A moment of quiet, a tiny gasp barely heard over the noise of the club, and she came. Milking me. Coating me in her sweet juice as I lapped up every drop. It was glorious and beautiful the way her legs shook, how the muscles inside squeezed my fingers in a rhythm as old as time. How her hips jerked and her knees seemed to melt. Completely and utterly perfect.

But still not enough.

CHAPTER TEN

Saturday Night

MY COCK WAS READY TO BURST.

Suddenly very aware of the possibility of people watching her, I rose to my feet between her and the table, practically holding her up as she sagged. She smiled up at me and wrapped her arms around my neck. That expression—her flushed, happy, postcoital look—was mine and mine alone. For the very first time in my very long life, I didn't want others to see her like that. I didn't want to share her. Ever.

Wrangling the new possessiveness flooding through me, I blocked her with my body and held her to my chest, supporting her as she came down from her high. Pressing my cock into her stomach to try to find some release from the pain of my need.

"Plum?"

"Yeah?" She leaned back, looking up at me, her

brow furrowing when she met my gaze. "What's wrong?"

I shook my head, stunned almost silent by my want. By my craving. "I don't want to do this here."

Her face pulled tight into a confused expression. "Then what do you want?"

Honest, open, I said the only thing I could. "I want to bury myself in your sweet pussy and make you come again. I want to feel you shatter on my cock. But not here. Not in front of these people."

Her hands gripped my arms, squeezing, holding me tighter. "You want to be alone with me?"

"Very much so, my dear. I can't handle the thought of these men seeing more of you than they already have."

Plum leaned back, smiling. "There's a door down that hallway. Want to see where it goes?"

I growled and spun us, keeping my arms around her as I directed us to the door. Plum laughed the whole way, stumbling a bit over my feet. The door swung open with ease, unlocked, a darkened supply closet hidden behind it. I pushed Plum inside and followed her, slamming the door behind me. Locking the cheap handle just in case.

"Did you see all those people, Plum?" I hissed, my fangs growing. I pressed her body against the shelves, her arms supporting her, my hips pressed against hers. "They watched you come, didn't they?"

She wiggled that delectable ass, one hand coming around to my hips to pull me closer. But she didn't speak. She held me, pulled me, teased my already too-hard cock. But her mouth stayed closed. I'd have to fix that.

"Answer me, Plum."

"Yes," she said, voice soft but strong.

"Did you know they were watching?"

"I caught the eye of one or two looking my way."

"You're a naughty girl, Plum. Your orgasm should be mine. I worked for it, earned it, and you gave it away." I smacked her ass, hard, enough to make her jump. She whimpered, pulling me closer, grasping at my pants.

"You'd like that, wouldn't you? Like to be spanked right here in our little corner. You want a little pain, Plum? Or do you want me to fuck that pretty pussy hard right here and now?"

"Yes," she hissed, trying to drag my hand between her legs.

"If I do this, Plum," I whispered, fighting back a smirk, knowing I had her, "I want it my way. I'll fuck you right here, make you come again on my cock, but by my rules."

"What rules?"

Instead of answering, I spun her, pressing her down until she picked up on my intentions. She hit her knees with grace, immediately reaching to unfasten my pants.

"Good girl, Plum. Suck me. Let me feel those lips on my cock."

I hissed when she pulled me out, loving the feel of her touch. Her eyes locked on mine as she stroked me, running her soft skin over mine. Base to tip, slowly driving me mad. Then she smirked before sitting back on her heels and licking her lips.

Opening her mouth for me.

"Fucking perfect, Plum." I pressed forward, sliding between those red lips of hers. Groaning as her hot, wet mouth surrounded me. "That's it. Take it all. Every inch."

Plum groaned, running her tongue along the underside of my cock. But she didn't move. She sat still as I pressed in again, pulling out almost to the tip, giving her the chance to run her tongue along the ridge before pushing back inside. Fuck, her mouth felt good. Felt amazing. And the way she sucked on me, the way she used her tongue and teeth to tease me, was positively divine. In and out, tongue teasing, a tiny choke every now and again when I went too deep. But she never let me go, never tried to back away. She took everything I had to give, even leaning forward for more. She worked me right to the edge, to the point that my balls pulled up tight and sparks tingled in my spine. Another minute, a couple more strokes, and I'd come down her throat.

But her mouth wasn't all I wanted.

Without preamble, I pulled out and yanked her to her feet. Spinning her, I pressed her against the shelves once more, pulling up her skirt. One hand ran over the fleshy cheek of her ass, kneading it, warming it up. The other slid around her hip, between her legs, and cupped her pussy. Owning it.

"Mine, naughty girl. No one's going to see the pleasure on your face again. From now on, it's all mine. It'll be my cock inside this sweet cunt. It'll be me fucking you until you shiver and quake. Would you like that, naughty girl?

She moaned as my fingers delved between her legs, pulling her open, massaging her clit as I knew she enjoyed. Teasing her until I could slide inside.

"Masterson," she groaned, leaning forward, tilting her hips to give me the perfect angle. My sweet, naughty Plum.

"Yes, beautiful?" I released my cock and covered myself with a condom in seconds, grabbing her hip and yanking her into the right position. Her height and the ridiculously high shoes she wore put her at the perfect level for this. I'd have to remember that. Have to buy her more shoes like the ones she wore so I could make sure she was always ready. Because tonight wouldn't be enough. No, my inner beast liked her too much, loved the sweetness of her blood and the softness of her pussy. Tonight would not be the end; it was only the beginning.

She shivered as I stroked the head of my cock through her wetness, bumping her clit on each glide. "Please."

I leaned down, nipped her neck, making her bleed, a tiny thread of red against her pale skin. A drop of sugary delight for me to enjoy. "As you wish."

Holding her tight, fingers still massaging her clit, I thrust into her pussy. No waiting, no edging my way inside. One push, forceful and demanding, and I was exactly where I'd been wanting to be. Hanging on to my control with everything I had, locking my body down so I didn't come right then. Plum yelped and scrambled to stay in place against the shelves as I leaned into her, making me smirk.

"If you let go," I growled in her ear, "I stop. You'll be stuck using your own fingers to get off tonight, Plum. Just like last night."

She froze, holding her breath, her body stiff. My grin was surely wicked at that point.

"That's right, sweet. I was there. Watching you. Did it feel good? Did your fingers feel all warm and soft up inside that cunt?" I leaned down, growling, placing my lips against her ear.

"My cock is inside you now, Plum. Does that feel better than my fingers? Better than yours?" I pushed in deep, grinding against her ass. "Is this what you were thinking about last night as you fucked yourself all alone? As those fingers made you come?"

Plum swallowed hard, groaning a "yes" as she squeezed her walls around my cock.

"Fucking tease," I hissed, sliding my hand down to smack her ass. "I'm going to give you what you want, Plum. So don't let go."

Her knuckles went white as she gripped the edges of the shelf. With my first good thrust, she spread her legs wider, tilting her ass up at me. Giving me the perfect position. And it was perfect. Hot and submissive and absolutely what I wanted. What I needed. Thrusting harder with each stroke, I pounded into her. Forcing her up on her toes. Squeezing her clit in a rhythm to match that of my cock.

Groaning, clinging to the shelf as if her life depended on that hold, Plum rode out my heavy fucking. Taking everything I had to give and practically demanding more with her body. Leaning over her, I nipped her ear again, licking the trail of blood and letting it sit on my tongue. Tasting her. Fuck, she was delicious. Almost as good as the taste of her pussy. Almost, but not quite. Which was how I knew I'd found my perfect donor. The one woman who could entice me in all ways, keep me satisfied. And damn it, I wanted to do the same for her.

"I'm going to bite you when I come, my sweet." I hissed and closed my eyes as her walls spasmed around me, both of us just about ready to go, ready to fall over that cliff. "Once you come on my cock, I'll let go, taking mine. And then I'll draw your blood into my mouth. Fucking taste you. It'll feel good, Plum. I promise."

"Yes," she moaned, tightening around my cock. Preparing. Ready to come. I pressed harder on her clit, wanting it, waiting. Needing to feel her before I could go.

Before I could say another word, I pinched her clit hard and thrust deep. She came with a yelp, her walls squeezing me like a vise. I faltered, my rhythm changing, still thrusting hard and fast into her as I came as well. Without thought, I struck, teeth driving deep into her neck, sucking hard on her skin, probably tearing her flesh. I was careful with what I took, though. I didn't want to drain her. No. My sweet Plum was too good to let go.

My thrusts slowed, lost their rhythm. I kept my arms around Plum, one hand covering her pussy, cupping it as I drank from her. Not long, just a few seconds. A few blessed mouthfuls before I stilled. Teeth in her neck, cock in her pussy. Completely connected. Owned. Mine.

Finished, both my hungers finally sated, I pulled completely out of my Plum. Keeping my arms around her and my hand between her legs. She leaned against the shelves, head on her arm as she panted, shivering every few breaths.

"Thank you, Plum," I whispered, kissing her cheek.

She hummed a slight giggling sound. "You're thanking me? That was the best orgasm of my life. I should be on my knees thanking you."

"Well, if you'd like…" I put a hand on her shoulder as if to push her down. She spun, laughing, grabbing my hips.

"You're insatiable."

"And you're mine." I leaned over to press a kiss to her lips. A gentle one. Something new for me. "My donor, my Plum."

She gave me a mock glare as she pulled back, tugging her skirt down. "Donor, huh? That sounds a bit permanent."

"Precisely."

"Don't you think you should know my name before you go taking ownership of my blood?"

"And your pussy. Don't neglect that fact. I want everything." I yanked her back into my arms, dropping another soft kiss to her lips. "So tell me, Plum. What's your name?"

"Vale. Doctor Vale Theroux, to be exact." She

tugged at her hair, straightening the silky waves before pulling her clothes back into place. "I should go find my friends. They'll be worried if I don't show my face again."

"Of course, though I do believe they're as occupied as you've been."

I opened the door for her and she stepped into the hall, eyebrows raised. "You know something I don't?"

I shrugged, leading her toward the dance floor. "I made sure some friends of mine kept them busy, that's all." I nodded toward the blonde she'd been with earlier, the one grinding on Samuelson.

Plum, or rather Vale, shook her head. "She is going to kill you."

"Doubtful." Before Vale could rush off to meet up with her friend, there was one more thing I needed to know. "What is it you do at the hospital, Dr. Theroux?"

She waved to her friend, who seemed almost sad to be interrupted. "I'm a medical examiner."

I stopped, frozen, staring. "A medical examiner?"

Vale grinned and backed away, heading for her friend who'd somehow escaped Samuelson's wandering hands. "Yeah. I autopsy dead people all day. Of course, being able to talk to them makes figuring out a cause of death much simpler."

I gaped, nearly dumbfounded. "You smelled like death."

"Well, of course I did. It's part of my charm." Her smile turned brighter, almost teasing me. I laughed and followed her onto the dance floor. Joining Samuelson and the blonde near the middle.

Ready to have a bit more fun before I stole my Plum away for another round.

EPILOGUE

Wednesday night, I sat outside Vale's window. Waiting. Wanting.

We'd met at the coffee shop every day since the club and had been spending much more time alone together. Well, not totally alone. I'd convinced her to join me in the bathroom Monday morning for a quick fuck over the sink. Looking into her eyes in the mirror as she came was one of my new favorite things. I needed to do it again, and soon.

Tuesday, she'd dragged me into the alley behind the building and shoved me into the wall, sucking my cock down in a move that had my eyes rolling back in my head. I'd fucked her mouth harder than I probably should have, gripping her head to hold her still and pushing into her throat. She'd taken it, taken every inch. And liked it. Letting me come down her throat as she swallowed. Positively divine.

But Vale had gone straight home tonight after work,

claiming to need time to shower before I arrived. So I relegated myself to sitting outside her window in the shadows and watching. Of course, being my Plum, she had to put on a show for me once she'd finished her bathing. She lay on her bed, her ass toward the window…legs bent and spread. Naked. Her fingers deep in her pussy as her other hand sped over her clit. Fucking herself.

I'd rather it be me.

I dissolved and reappeared inside her bedroom, standing next to her bed. Her eyes met mine as if I wasn't expected, as if I'd surprised her. Not that I thought for a second that was true. She could feel me as much as I could feel her, sense me coming near. She knew I'd been outside watching as she'd dropped the towel after her shower and started playing with herself. Knew how much I enjoyed this game.

"Enjoying yourself, Plum?"

"I was waiting for you," she said, her voice all breathy and strained.

"This isn't waiting. This is moving ahead with me." I smiled, letting my hand wander down her thigh, rubbing my fingers over the back of hers. "Though you seem to be doing a good job yourself. You're quite wet and swollen."

"You'd do it better."

I slid a finger under her hand, circling her clit. "Would I now?"

"Masterson," she groaned. "Please."

"Please what, Plum?"

"Please do something."

I dropped to my knees, pulling her hands away from herself, spreading her wider for me. Beautiful and wet, her pussy called for me. Ready for my attention. I ran a fingernail along the seam of her thigh, cutting her, making her bleed just enough to tease my senses. The bright red ran down as gravity pulled it, mixing with where she was already wet along her upper thighs, where she dripped and glistened from what she'd been doing. A combination of blood and arousal that made my mouth water.

"I want your pussy more than your blood tonight, beautiful. But I'll take both."

She quirked a smile. "Lucky for me."

I licked over her clit, slipping my tongue inside her with a groan before pulling away. "I think I'm the lucky one."

She lay back, watching me, letting me lick and pet and play. "Just don't take so much this time. I was practically anemic the last three days."

Letting my fangs lengthen, showing her my predator side, I pushed her knees farther apart. "As you wish."

Fingers sliding into her pussy, thumb pressing on her clit, I bit into her thigh, purposely hitting the femoral artery. Making her come. Making her scream. Making her mine.

ALSO BY ELLIS LEIGH

———

FERAL BREED MOTORCYCLE CLUB

Wolf shifters, motorcycles, witches, and a threat
lurking in the shadows.

Novels

Claiming His Fate

Claiming His Need

Claiming His Witch

Claiming His Beauty

Claiming His Fire

Claiming His Desire

Collections

Claiming Their Forever: A Collection of Shorts

———

FERAL BREED FOLLOWINGS

Stand-alone stories of characters first met in the

Feral Breed Motorcycle Club series. Featuring cage fighters, dragon shifters, second chances, and young love.

Claiming His Chance

Claiming His Prize

———

THE GATHERING TALES

Come and enjoy tales from the biggest shifter event of the year as wolves from around the country fall in lust, in love, and in fate at The Gathering.

Killian and Lyra

Gideon and Kalie

Blasius, Dante, and Moira

Homecoming

Also available in one convenient anthology in both electronic and paperback formats.

The Gathering Tales

———

THE DEVIL'S DIRES

There's no escaping a Dire Wolf on the hunt…

Savage Surrender

Savage Sanctuary

Savage Seduction

Savage Silence

Savage Sacrifice

———

Motor City Alien Mail Order Brides

Where the men aren't human and the women are
uninformed.

Cutlass

Hudson

Maverick

———

Stand-Alone Romance

Bearly Dreaming: A Southern Shifters Worlds Novella

Masterson: A Vampire Sons Story

ABOUT THE AUTHOR

A storyteller from the time she could talk, Ellis grew up among family legends of hauntings, psychics, and love spanning decades. Those stories didn't always have the happiest of endings, so they inspired her to write about real life, real love, and the difficulties therein. From farmers to werewolves, store clerks to witches—if there's love to be found, she'll write about it. Ellis lives in the Chicago area with her husband, daughters, and two tiny fish that take up way too much of her time.

www.ellisleigh.com/newsletter

———

http://www.ellisleigh.com
ellis@ellisleigh.com
https://www.facebook.com/ellisleighwrites
https://twitter.com/ellis_writes

CPSIA information can be obtained
at www.ICGtesting.com
Printed in the USA
FSOW02n2353140317
31712FS

9 781944 336226